To Nadia, Karin, Olivia and Alain

Irene Ritter
Amos and Bertha, the Dragons of Mount Pilatus
Adapted from a local legend
Told and illustrated by Irene Ritter

Design: Irene Bucher, Lucerne, Switzerland

All rights reserved

First edition 1999, second edition 2003, third edition 2007

Printed by Gamma Druck + Verlag AG, Altdorf/Uri, Switzerland

© 2007 Gamma Druck + Verlag AG, Altdorf/Uri, Switzerland

ISBN 978-3-906200-25-5

AMOS AND BERTHA
THE DRAGONS
OF MOUNT PILATUS
adapted from a local legend

Told and illustrated
by Irene Ritter

WHERE THE DRAGONS LIVE

Once upon a time,
long long ago,
two dragons lived in a cave
on a high mountain in the
middle of Switzerland.
Their names were
Amos and Bertha.
Amos was a handsome
dragon, tall and thin.
A little vain, too. He spent
a lot of time polishing the bright
green scales all the way down his back and tail. Amos
always made sure his silver-grey belly was groomed
to perfection. Most of all he took great pride
in his beautiful big green wings.

Bertha was not exactly fat.
She was just nicely plump.
Like her wings, the scales on
her back shone with a touch
of purple which set off her
pretty pink belly. She was
a cheerful dragon. Sparks
flickered in her eyes and
little flames danced on her
tongue when she sang.

Amos and Bertha's home was called Mount Pilatus. Like a huge grey castle, this mountain guarded the shore of a long lake. Winds howled and moaned around its jagged peaks. Storms raged with fireworks of lightning, as thunder boomed off the rock walls and bullets of hail went pelting into the valleys below.

The people who lived in the valleys were terrified when this happened. They believed evil spirits haunted the mountain and blamed them for the dreadful storms. Many strange stories told of great mischief done by ghosts, goblins, witches and dragons. Yet nobody had ever really seen a dragon close up.

Bertha and Amos were the only dragons who lived on Mount Pilatus. When they spread their wings, a blaze of orange fire enveloped them as they rose into the sky. The quicker they flew, the brighter glowed the whirls of heat round their bodies and the flames leaping off their breath. Whenever the farmers and townspeople saw these fiery creatures, they ran away to hide.

It was said that an awful fate awaited anyone lost on the heights of Mount Pilatus in fog or dark of night. So only few people were brave enough to climb the mountain where Amos and Bertha lived.

SEPPI

One man had no fear of Mount Pilatus. He was a cooper, a maker of casks, who lived in Lucerne, the market-town at the foot of the mountain. The high quality of his work earned him an excellent reputation among the wine and beer merchants. To make the hoops, the circular bands of wood binding the staves of his casks, he used the strong flexible branches off trees that grew high up on the mountain.

The cooper had a son called Seppi. He was twelve years old and a strong, plucky boy. He helped in the workshop, which he enjoyed more than school. He loved to climb with his father to the topmost forests and very soon learned where to find the right kind of branches.

One day, when winter already nipped the air, the cooper took to his bed with a high fever. He was so ill, he could not climb up Mount Pilatus to gather the hoop-wood. He needed to replenish his supply to carry him through with his work until the spring.

Seppi pleaded with his father to let him go alone. The cooper would not hear of it. He was very worried about all the dangers that might be lurking on the mountain. But the boy promised to be careful and in the end his father gave in.

Pride shone in Seppi's brown eyes. He laced up his mountain boots and put on his warmest clothes. He wrapped the thick red scarf his mother had knitted him

for his birthday round his neck and pulled the matching woollen cap over his dark curls. With his parents' blessing and a big kiss from his mother, he was ready. Whistling with excitement, Seppi slung his haversack and his father's bags over his shoulders and set out.

Under a deep blue sky the mountain seemed to glow in a last show of alpine lushness. Here and there autumn crocus still raised lilac heads on the meadows. Next to a stream, where it formed a pool sparkling with the golden noonday sun, Seppi sat on a rock to eat the bread and cheese he had taken along. The piece of cake his mother had baked, he kept for later, to eat on his way home.

Cupping his hands in the pool, he took a few sips of the icy water. Then he ate his apple and waited a moment longer to listen to the birdcalls echoing on the mountain walls. Seppi was good at imitating birds and was tempted to play with the echo. But he knew that daylight now was short.

So Seppi, being a good boy and remembering his father's words, continued on his way. He was careful to avoid the bogs hidden by carpets of green moss. Rounding a bend, he stopped and stood quite still, holding his breath. Above him, poised on the edge of a cliff was a mountain goat. For a moment they looked at each other. Then in a scuttle of hooves, it was gone.

ON THE MOUNTAIN

Seppi felt happy and adventurous as he climbed higher and higher. His father had taught him the way through the deep ravines, the open meadowland and thick forests. But he was so intent in his search for the right trees from which to cut the wood, that he did not pay much attention to where he was going.

Suddenly the boy realised that he had strayed far off the path. Where was he? It was getting dark. Wisps of evening mist distorted the view. He could not recognize any familiar landmarks. Bats swished into the gathering dusk. All his daring left him. His one thought now was to get home safely before night fell. An owl hooted nearby. Fighting down his fear, Seppi picked up his loads and scrambled down. In his haste he forgot how treacherous the mountain could be.

Seppi's feet slipped on the rocks.

His bags and the loads of branches fell down the cliffs and were lost. He clutched at shrubs. The twigs broke. He slid faster and faster down the rock face, until he plunged into a deep dark hole.

As he fell, Seppi remembered a prayer his mother had taught him and he begged his guardian angel to save him. The prayer was answered for he landed on something soft and warm. He was not even hurt!

It was pitch black in the hole. Weird muffled sounds made Seppi sick with fear. The soft warm thing he had landed on moved and grunted. His heart beat loudly as he felt around him. Suddenly his hands met a strange rough surface.

As his eyes grew accustomed to the darkness, it seemed that he was lying on top of a mound. The mound was huge. On both sides he discovered flat spiky layers. He looked down and saw a long row of scales all the way to the end of what appeared to be a tail. In the opposite direction, a shred of smoke rose from a long snout. Then he understood. He was lying on a dragon! Seppi knew of the two dragons of Mount Pilatus – but on which one had he landed?

IN THE CAVE

Bertha was fast asleep in the cave when Seppi dropped on her. She had only vaguely stirred. But Amos had noticed something and went over to Bertha to see what had tumbled down. A smell of sulphur made Seppi turn his head. To his horror, he saw Amos peering at him with fiery eyes and flames streaming from his nostrils. He choked and fainted.

Seppi found himself lying on the cave floor when he came round. It was a long time since he had eaten and his stomach rumbled painfully. Tears were not far away. He remembered the piece of cake in his pocket and took it out. It was badly squashed. He quickly stuffed some of it into his mouth.

Amos came to sniff the rest of the cake. With trembling fingers Seppi broke a bit off and held it out to him. Amos licked it and then swallowed it. Bertha got up and came to see what there was to eat. Hoping she would not eat him, Seppi gave her his last piece. She gobbled it and then went to lick the rock face at a place where a white creamy liquid oozed out.

Amos tugged at the boy's sleeve and pulled him to the rock. Seppi watched Amos lick the wall and tried it too. The milky substance was salty but satisfying. He was not hungry any more.

Feeling a little safer, Seppi began to look around. He saw he was in a fairly big cave. The entrance was above a high, slippery rock wall and he could not imagine how he would ever get up there. The light at the top was very dim. A musty, slightly sour smell hung in the air.

Seppi supposed he must have fallen into the Moonmilk Cave. He had heard of this moonmilk that was scraped off the rock walls and used as a remedy for various ailments. He strained to listen for the sound of cowbells that people said you could hear from inside the Moonmilk Cave. But soon he realized that there were no cows any more because it was nearly wintertime. However, the thought of being able to lick moonmilk in the company of these two kindly dragons comforted him.

A draught of wind made him pull his jacket closer. He huddled shivering on the cave floor. The cold made him feel lonely. Remembering the softness of Bertha's belly, Seppi cautiously went to touch her. The fire inside her made her body wonderfully warm. Gratefully he cuddled up to her.

Days and nights went by. The dragons slept most of the time and did not seem to mind Seppi's presence. Snug with warmth and moonmilk, the boy soon lost all count of time and drifted into a deep sleep.

SPRINGTIME

One day, Amos got up. He sniffed the air with excitement. Puffing and snorting, he pushed himself up onto the ledge at the entrance. After taking several deep breaths, he started to preen himself. His wings quivered and flashed in the bright sun, the tips of his scales spangling the cave with green glitter. Finally, with a satisfied grunt, Amos spread his wings and flew off.

Seppi realized that the light was different. It had become much brighter. Spring must have come. He turned to Bertha to see what she would do. She too got up. She nudged and fussed around him. He had no idea what she wanted. He watched her go up to the entrance. All of a sudden he had a terrible thought: how was he going to get out of the cave?

When Bertha had finished sprucing herself up, she sang a tune, over and over, lolling from side to side on the ledge. Seppi had never heard such a strange sound. He stood on the cave floor listening to her, spellbound.

Suddenly, looking down at him, she grunted, grunted… and grunted. The boy still did not understand what she wanted. So Bertha turned round. She put her tail down the cave opening. When Seppi grabbed hold of it, he was immediately lifted onto the rock ledge outside. "Yipee!" he shouted, jumping up and down with joy at seeing the sun again.

Then he sat once more astride Bertha's tail and off they flew, over the bay of Lucerne, on to the town.

When the townspeople saw this dragon coming straight at them, they dropped everything and ran away to hide wherever possible. Those inquisitive or brave enough to peep, saw the dragon land on the market square and a boy get off its tail. They recognized Seppi, the cooper's son, and stared in open-mouthed amazement on seeing him stroke the dragon and wave as it flew off. As soon as the dragon was gone, everyone ran out clamouring for Seppi to tell of his adventure.

But Seppi ran home. His mother opened the door. On seeing the son she had thought lost forever, she gave a cry of joy, gathering him into her arms. Tears of relief streamed down her cheeks. Both were laughing and crying as they hugged. His younger brothers and sisters hopped and skipped happily around them.

All winter long, the cooper had bitterly reproached himself for having allowed his son to go up the mountain alone. Now he was greatly relieved, but also very proud of Seppi for having survived this adventure so well. He wanted all those around him to share in his happiness, so he invited everyone to a meal at the inn next door. The innkeeper renamed it "The Dragons' Cave" in Seppi's honour and the boy had to tell his story again and again.

From then on the townspeople no longer ran away whenever the dragons flew overhead. They stopped to look up and marvel at Amos and Bertha, because now they knew that they were kindly creatures.

Seppi painted portraits of the two dragons and hung the pictures over his bed. Every day he gazed at Mount Pilatus to catch a glimpse of pink and purple and shining green wings.

Amos, Bertha and Seppi remained friends ever after.

The author

When Irene Ritter looks out her window, Mount Pilatus fills the view. Living on the shore of the Lake of Lucerne for well over thirty years, she has become familiar with the many changes of mood so special to this mountain.

Irene Ritter was born in France, her mother was Russian, her father was French, she grew up in England, married a Swiss and settled in Switzerland. She has two children and four grandchildren. Fluent in several languages, she put them to good use working in London for the BBC and international organizations. In Lucerne she became a freelance broadcaster and feature writer in English on the Swiss way of life. She now enjoys writing fiction.

Special thanks to Gérard Ryan for editing the manuscript.